Beauty and the Beast

Beauty and the Beast

by Marianna Mayer
pictures by Mercer Mayer

Sea Star Books
NEW YORK

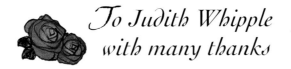

To Judith Whipple with many thanks

Text copyright © 1978 by Marianna Mayer.
Illustrations copyright © 1978 by Mercer Mayer.
First published by Four Winds Press / Scholastic, Inc., New York, 1978.

Published in the United States by SEASTAR BOOKS,
a division of NORTH-SOUTH BOOKS INC., New York.
Library of Congress Cataloging-in-Publication Data is available.

ISBN 1-58717-017-5 (trade binding)
1 3 5 7 9 TB 10 8 6 4 2
ISBN 1-58717-018-3 (library binding)
1 3 5 7 9 LB 10 8 6 4 2
601920168
Printed by Proost N.V. in Belgium.

For more information about our books, and the authors and artists who create them, visit our web site: www.northsouth.com

There once was a wealthy merchant who lived with his three daughters and three sons. His wife had died long before, but his children filled his life and his business gave him little time to be lonely.

One day, a great storm came up, destroying all the merchant's ships and their rich cargo. The merchant was desolate. How could he tell his children of this terrible misfortune? Now they must sell all they had. They would have to move from their comfortable house in the city to a modest one he owned in the country. It would be a very different life. His children would no longer have servants to wait on them. Instead, the family would spend their time working their small fields, living off what the land would provide.

"All our ships have been lost in the storm!" the merchant told his children that night. "We will have to work very hard from now on to manage just small necessities."

All the children complained loudly except for Beauty, the merchant's youngest daughter. Of all his daughters, she was the most like her mother. She loved the country best of all, as her mother had. Trying to cheer them, she said, "Don't worry, Father. You'll see—it will be a new life for us. I will love to live in the country. It will be as though we were having our vacation all year long."

Beauty's sisters frowned at her. "How very stupid you are!" they told her, outraged. "How will we ever find husbands? Do you think we've been brought up to marry farmers?" Beauty's sisters were very proud and beautiful, and considered themselves too good for most of the rich noblemen who had already asked for their hand in marriage. Now their prospects seemed dim indeed.

While their brothers and Beauty sorted out what would be sold and what would be kept, the two sisters sulked and complained to their sad father. But their father was firm. So go they did, but they continued to sulk and did as little as possible to help with any of the chores. "I can't wash dishes. That's servants' work. How will I ever find a husband if my hands are rough and red?" said one. "And I can't possibly help in the fields. That's men's work. What would my friends think if they happened by?"

So Beauty and her three brothers were kept busy doing all the chores. They would say, "Well, the girls aren't strong. And Beauty is different. After all, she does love the country. She is so good with the animals."

Beauty would just smile, for she never thought to complain. In a way it was true that she didn't mind the work. She very much wanted her father to see that they could indeed manage. So she stayed out in the fields helping her brothers, while her sisters complained that the work wasn't fit for a lady. Beauty proved them wrong, for she was every bit as graceful and lovely as her sisters. But hard work never seemed to discourage her.

At night, too tired to read her favorite books, she would go quietly to bed. But she loved the country and the look of pride in her father's eyes was reward enough for her.

One day, a friend arrived from the city with the news that some of the merchant's ships were reported washed up in a nearby port. Everyone was filled with hope, and the sisters were convinced they would all be rich again. As their father packed for his journey, they planned what they wanted him to bring back as gifts for them.

"Bring us dresses of silk and fine shoes and a carriage to ride in, so that when we return to the city everyone will marvel at us."

"Very well," said the hopeful merchant. "You shall have the finest dresses money can buy. But what do you want me to bring to you, Beauty?"

Beauty had been very quiet while her sisters planned. She gathered her father's traveling clothes and put them into his small trunk. "Really, there is nothing I ," she said, sad to see her father go.

"Now, you must have something you'd like me to bring you. Tell me, girl, what shall it be?"

"Oooh," her sisters groaned. "What could Beauty possibly want? She's so happy here." They both laughed.

Beauty saw her father frown. To put an end to the discussion she said, "Yes, there is something I'd love to have. Please bring me back a rose. We never see any here."

"Oh, what a stupid present that is," said her sisters.

"I'll bring you back the very best rose, my dear," said her father as he kissed them all good-bye. Then he rode off on his horse with his friend.

When they arrived at the port it was their sad task to survey what was left of the rich cargo. Most of it was badly damaged and the few valuables that were salvaged had been confiscated by bill collectors. So there was nothing to be joyful about. The trip was a failure. After sadly bidding farewell to his trusted friend, the merchant set out for home.

Late in the night he lost his way. Dusk fell in the forest, and the gloomy night became more and more threatening. A storm began to wake in the dark sky. It twisted the clouds and growled terrible thunder. Rain turned to snow, and the shivering merchant began to look for shelter from the night. Cold, tired, and hungry, he came upon a brightly lighted palace. The gates leading to its doors were open, and smoke billowed from every chimney.

"Perhaps," thought the weary merchant, "the owner of this fine palace wouldn't mind allowing a tired and lost traveler a bit of warmth by his fire."

When the merchant approached he found the doors open, and he entered. Before him he saw a grand hall, with a warm glowing fire in the fireplace. To his surprise, he saw a table set for one before the fireplace, with steaming hot soup, freshly baked bread, and what looked like a delicious meat pie. He called out, but no one replied, so he sat down before it. "I don't suppose I should help myself," he thought as he ate. But he was exhausted and hunger had gotten the best of his sense. So he told himself that perhaps the meal was meant for him, or some other lost and tired traveler. Instead of being suspicious, he took comfort in it.

After finishing the food, the merchant went out in search of his horse, which he found grazing comfortably in the nearby stable on a great heap of sweet hay. Again this did not cause him suspicion. Instead, he returned to the warmth of the palace and finished the fine wine that accompanied his meal. But he was too fatigued to continue on his journey. "Surely it can't hurt to linger just a bit longer," he thought between yawns. "Perhaps when I wake, the kind master of this palace will have returned and I may have an opportunity to thank him for his hospitality. Certainly it couldn't do any harm to remain."

He fell into a peaceful and enchanted sleep. When he woke in the morning, he found himself in a beautiful bed with silk sheets in a room fit for royalty. There at his bedside was a tray laid out with sweet rolls and hot porridge, milk, tea, and honey. "Goodness, the master of this house is a generous man," he thought.

After finishing his breakfast he dressed hurriedly, eager to go out on the grounds to see if he might find at least one servant, or even the master himself. But he found no one.

The merchant was puzzled. Surely there would at least be servants to manage a palace of this size! Growing more and more nervous, the merchant quickly passed through the garden, stopping only to glance at some especially beautiful roses. He remembered Beauty's wish for a single rose and without thinking, he hastily broke one from the bush.

Suddenly a roar shook the entire garden. Stricken with fear, the merchant fell to his knees and covered his head with his arms. When the roaring stopped, the merchant looked up to behold a most hideous beast.

"How dare you steal one of my roses?" he growled.

"Please, Master, had I known that this rose was precious to you I never would have taken it," the merchant cried.

The beast was dressed in clothes fit for a prince, but his face was that of a wild animal. The terrified merchant could barely look at him without shuddering. Hoping the beast would take pity on him he told his story, ending with Beauty's request for a single rose.

"I gave you shelter and food. But you repay this by stealing from me. Prepare to die for your thievery!" the beast roared.

The merchant pleaded with the beast, begging for his children, who would be orphaned should he die. Finally the beast was softened enough to bargain.

"If your daughter loves you enough to come in your place I will take her instead. If she refuses you will return to me to take your punishment."

"I would never allow my daughter to take my place!" protested the merchant. "Kill me if you must." But the beast refused.

"It must be your daughter's choice. If she will not come then at least go to your family and say good-bye. If you do not return I will come and find you."

The merchant agreed on his honor to return in three days.

"Go into my palace and take the chest I have left for you," the beast told him. "You will find your horse waiting at the gate and a horse for your daughter's return. But remember, Merchant, if you do not return I will hunt you down."

When the merchant arrived home his children were delighted to see him. They opened the chest the beast had given them to find it filled with silver. When the merchant told them of the bargain he had made with the beast, however, they wept. All but Beauty, who was determined that her father should not die.

"I will go to the beast in your place, Father. I am sure no harm will come to me."

Beauty's brothers leaped up, determined to go to the palace and kill the beast, while her sisters forced big false tears from their eyes and wailed about losing Beauty. In their hearts, they thought about how they would not miss her at all.

No matter how her father and brothers protested, Beauty insisted. She had made up her mind—she would go to live with the beast. "It is my fault that all this has happened to you, Father. I will stay with the beast. Surely he can't be as bad as you think. He has spared you and given us this treasure. My staying with him is a small price to pay for all his kindness."

Finally the day came for the merchant to return with his daughter. Up to the last moment her brothers pleaded with her to let them go back and attempt to slay the beast, but Beauty refused. She was convinced the beast would not harm any of them if only they did as he had commanded.

The beast's horse led Beauty and her father back to the palace. Again it was night, and the palace glowed with light. It seemed more beautiful than the merchant had remembered it. When they entered, the dining table was again set before the fire, but this time it was set for two. As filled with fear as the travelers were, they were still tired and hungry. They seated themselves at the table.

"Surely this is the finest meal I've ever had, Father. How kind this lord is to have thought of our needs."

Beauty's father looked at her lovingly, saying nothing, only thinking of how frightened his daughter would be once she finally met the master of this house.

At last, the beast entered from the garden. "Good evening, Merchant. It was good of you to come as we agreed. And you, Beauty, are certainly a brave young woman. She must love you dearly, Merchant, to have come."

Beauty bowed her head in greeting to the beast. "How very frightening he is," she thought, "and yet his eyes are so sad. He must be very lonely, living in this large palace all alone."

"We have come as you asked," said the merchant. "I have not been able to persuade my daughter to stay at home. But I plead with you to spare her, for I fear that you will deal harshly with her."

But the beast had no unkind words for either of them. Instead he asked, "Beauty, will you remain with me in my palace?"

"Yes, my lord, I will," Beauty answered, bowing her head.

"In this palace you alone are the mistress. All will do your bidding, including myself. You may refer to me as Beast, for that is what I am and I ask only that we speak the truth here." Turning to the merchant, who was astonished at the beast's

gentleness toward his daughter, the beast said, "You, Merchant, shall stay the night, but you must leave by morning. Take with you those three chests that you and your daughter may fill with gold to bring back to your family. And now I bid you good night." The beast bowed politely to Beauty and was gone.

Again the merchant begged Beauty to reconsider, and again she refused. So they stayed up till dawn, filling the chests with the gold and precious jewels. The more they filled the chests, the more room there was.

"Surely the beast is making fools of us both. My horse will never be able to carry such tremendous weight," the merchant said. But in the morning the merchant's horse stood at the gate with all three chests tied to the saddle.

Now at last it was time for the merchant to leave. Beauty kissed him good-bye, trying to conceal her tears. He finally set out, and in moments he was gone from view.

Then Beauty was alone. She walked slowly back into the palace, and went to her room. There she found the closets filled with beautiful clothes. Her dresser spilled over with jewels of every kind. As she exchanged her shabby dress for a fine silk one, she thought, "The beast will be pleased to see me wearing his gifts." Then she set out to explore the palace.

At the top of a long, winding staircase she found a tower room. It was circular, and filled with light. Every window looked out into the gardens below. In one corner was a large silver music box that played, when the lid was lifted, a continuously changing melody. On the bookshelves there were books of every kind bound in the finest leather. And in a small gilt cage was a tiny red bird that sang to her.

Beauty thought, "This is the most wonderful room in the palace. Poor beast, with all his wealth and love of beautiful things, he is wretched and lonely. Well, I will try to help him be happy."

Each day Beauty returned to the tower. She read many of the books. Often she would take the little bird from its cage, letting it fly free. Though the windows were open wide, it would never leave the tower. "Little bird, you are like me," she said. The bird flew to her shoulder, and rubbed its smooth beak gently against Beauty's cheek.

Every evening Beauty would have her dinner before the fire and the beast would join her. It was the only time she saw him. One of the first evenings in the palace Beauty asked, "Where do you spend your days, Beast?"

"Do not ask me, Beauty," was his reply.

"Please tell me what you do," she persisted.

The beast looked at her and a great sorrow filled his face. But just as quickly his expression changed to anger. He raised his rough fur-covered claws and answered, "I hunt. I prowl the woods for prey. I am an animal after all, my lady! I must kill for my meat. Unlike you I cannot eat gracefully."

Beauty was horrified. Her eyes filled with tears, and she looked away from his terrible gaze. "How very sad," was all she could say.

The beast left her with an abrupt good night.

Beauty ceased to ask questions that might hurt or embarrass the beast. At first she tried hard not to notice how frightening he looked. As time passed she found him so kind toward her that her fear left her.

"This palace is now yours, Beauty, and I am your slave," the beast told her one night.

During those evenings they would talk of many things, of magic and of the world. The beast knew many stories of foreign places and Beauty loved to hear him speak of them. His tales were so vivid she felt she was there herself. Beauty soon came to realize the beast was a magician as well. Often while telling a story he would wave his arm and a picture would unfold before their eyes. The characters in the story would move as real people and when the tale was over the players would bow and curtsy, then disappear. Many of the stories were funny, and Beauty and the beast would laugh together until the beast would remember he was a beast; then he would end the story quickly, bidding her good night. Before he left her he would always ask, "Beauty, will you be my wife?"

Beauty always replied the same way. "No, Beast. I am sorry, but though you are kind to me and have treated me fairly, I can never be your wife because I do not love you."

Then the beast would leave Beauty and she would want to weep for him.

Beauty most of all looked forward to the nights. When she went to bed, her sleep was filled with dreams lovelier than those she had ever had before. They were always the same. She would be in the garden of the palace near a shimmering

pond, the air was filled with the scent of roses, and her little red bird would fly about her singing the sweetest song. A handsome young prince would come and sit by her side. He seemed somehow familiar to Beauty, though she knew she had never seen him.

"Someday, Beauty, we will be together always." But then the dream would change and he would be gone. In his place she would hear a woman's voice speaking to her, "Look deep into others' beauty to find your happiness."

And Beauty would think to herself, "What does it mean? Why can't my prince be with me now?"

Those dreams melted into her days at the palace. She would look for her prince in the garden, and by the pond, but she never found him. Yet in her dreams he would tell her of his life.

"When I was a boy I was very vain and quite proud. My palace was filled with servants and everyone honored me and did my bidding. One day an old hag came begging at my palace gate. I showed her no pity, she was so ugly. The sight of her did not move me and I sent her away without food or money. As she left she warned that I would spend the rest of my life wandering in my fine palace without a friend till someone could find beauty in me. I laughed at her, but when I returned to my palace, I found it empty. I have been alone ever since."

When Beauty awoke she would tell herself that it was just a dream. But if it was, then how could she ever set the prince free?

One night, after having dinner with the beast, he again asked her the same question he always asked, and again she answered as kindly as she could, "No, Beast, I am sorry, but I can never be your wife because I do not love you." When he left her, the beast seemed sadder than ever before. Beauty went to her room eager to dream of her prince, but he did not appear. She stood before the pond calling to him, but instead an old woman approached her.

"Your prince cannot return to you, Beauty," she said. "Since he has failed to make you his wife, you must not really love him." Then she was gone.

"But I do," said Beauty.

Now Beauty had only the memory of the prince to comfort her.

The next morning when Beauty entered the tower, she found a small oval mirror. She looked into it, and there she saw her father lying ill, with her sisters and her brothers gathered around him.

That night at dinner, Beauty told the beast about the mirror. "It is a magic mirror," he told her. "If one is pure of heart, one can see into it. If you have seen your father there, then he must truly be ill."

"Please, Beast, let me go to him. If I could see him just for a little while, I know he would be better."

"You are a good daughter, Beauty. I cannot refuse you anything, for I am your slave. Take the mirror tomorrow, and simply will yourself by your father's side. Your wish will be granted. But please remember your poor beast who loves you, and return to me in three weeks."

Beauty was overjoyed. Still, when it came time for the beast to leave her and he again asked her to marry him, she could only say no to his request.

"Then good-bye, Beauty. Remember your promise to return to me in three weeks, for I will not live without you."

That night Beauty dreamed again of the garden and the shimmering pond. She looked for the prince but he was not there. Instead she saw the old woman. "How blind you are! I had hoped you would know that happiness comes from seeing what does not always lie on the surface. Some things are not on the surface at all."

The next day Beauty looked into the magic mirror, wishing with all her heart to be with her father. Instantly the handsome black horse that had led her to the palace called out to her from outside. Taking the mirror with her, she rushed to the gates of the palace and they were off.

The black horse galloped so fast Beauty barely felt the ground beneath them. In what seemed like moments she was back at her father's home. Though her father

was now very rich, thanks to the beast, he chose to remain in the country. When Beauty arrived, he was indeed very ill. Although he had servants to tend to his needs, they could not take Beauty's place. As soon as she was there caring for him, he began to recover rapidly.

When her sisters saw how well Beauty looked they were very envious. "Why was she so lucky?" they asked each other. Though the two had married well, they still felt resentful that their simple little sister lived in a beautiful palace like a queen, even if she did have to share it with a beast.

They decided to urge Beauty to stay. She could look after their father much better than the servants, and he was doing so well since her return. Certainly the beast would understand that her father needed her much more than he. On and on they connived, succeeding in making Beauty agree to at least stay longer than she had said she could. Later they giggled together thinking how angry the beast would be with her for disobeying him.

Beauty worried about the beast, but she could not bring herself to leave, for her father was so happy to have her with him.

After a time, Beauty had another dream. There again was the palace garden and the pond. Winter was setting in, the leaves were falling, and the sky was dark. On the ground lay the beast, looking quite dead. Beauty woke chilled, and filled with dread.

"My poor beast—how awful I have
been to him. How could I have betrayed
my promise when he's been so kind." She
said good-bye to her father, and immedi-
ately held the mirror before her, wishing
to be back at the palace. Again, the black
horse appeared; again the two galloped
with great speed to the palace. At the
pond was her beast, just as in her dream.
He looked quite dead.

Beauty knelt beside him, cradling his head in her arms.

"My poor beast, this is my fault for being so heartless. I have repaid your love with my own blindness and selfishness. Please recover. If you do, I swear to be your wife. I do love you."

The beast was not dead, but only weak with misery from the loss of her. As Beauty spoke, he stirred, and moved his great head. Before Beauty's eyes, he began to grow stronger. With each breath he took, his beastly appearance began to fade. Hearing his heart still beating, Beauty took some water from the pond and wet his dry lips. But she pulled back in surprise, for her beast was gone and in his place the prince of her dreams lay in her arms.

"You have released me from my enchantment, Beauty. If you will still consent to marry me, although I am no longer your beast, I promise I will always love you.

"Now at last I am free to tell you that the old woman was really a fairy in disguise sent to test me. Though I failed she was kind enough to put my whole palace in a magical spell till I could find you to redeem me. Say you will marry me and you shall be my queen."

At last Beauty understood the mystery of her dreams. The prince and the beast were one, and her love had saved them both from their enchantment.

The palace sang out with rejoicing. All the servants, noblemen, and fine ladies were freed from the spell of invisibility, and a great feast was prepared for the wedding.

So the prince and Beauty were married, and lived with love and happiness.
As for her sisters, well, you can imagine just how envious they felt of their little
sister's happiness.